IS THIS MY LAST STOP
FOR LOVE

IS THIS MY LAST STOP
FOR LOVE

L E S T E R   E D W A R D S

IS THIS MY LAST STOP FOR LOVE

iUniverse books may be ordered through booksellers or by contacting:

iUniverse
1663 Liberty Drive
Bloomington, IN 47403
www.iuniverse.com
1-800-Authors (1-800-288-4677)

ISBN: 978-1-4917-4689-9 (sc)
ISBN: 978-1-4917-4690-5 (e)

Print information available on the last page.

iUniverse rev. date: 09/10/2014

PLACE: TUPELO, MISSISSIPPI IN THE EARLY 1940'S 1942

T he sky was bright on a full moon night about two o'clock am. It was very quiet in the sharecroppers' quarters. In the faint distance, the sound of a newborn baby cries. Jim and his wife Jewel just had their first baby — an eight pound six ounce girl. Very pretty chocolate brown skin, hair straight like a mixed breed of Black and Indian. Jim, standing outside the door, rushes into the room when he hears the baby cry. As he entered, the midwife was carefully cutting the umbilical cord separating mother and baby. Jim stood there watching in awe.

Jim thought to himself, my first baby a beautiful little girl, a princess. My beautiful princess, that's gonna be her name — Princess. He leaned over and kissed Jewel, her face dribbling with sweat from the new birth. He told her how beautiful she was and she managed a smile as a sharp pain went through her stomach. The midwife prepared for the afterbirth. She asked Jim to leave the room, until the baby was cleaned up and his wife's stomach was wrapped around with a special cloth to keep down the stretch marks. Jim slowly backed out of the room with a big wide grin on his face and quietly closed the door. He walked outside, looked up at the full moon and let out loud yell, "Thank you Jesus, thank you Lord, thank you Holy Ghost." He rolled up a Prince Albert cigarette, called him back into the room.

Jennie, the midwife, cleaned up the baby washing her carefully making sure that the cord was sewed up. She then wrapped the baby in a small quilt and handed the baby to the mother. Jewel holds her new baby in her arms and the midwife says, "Oh, what a fine baby girl. Jennie, she is beautiful. Here's some chamomile tea, drink this it will help you to sleep." The midwife calls her daughter Joan to help her clean up all the mess. When they finished cleaning up, Jennie washed her hands and changed clothes. Then she sits down by the bed, eats a little bit of food and rears back in the rocking chair and closes her eyes. It's been a long night. She sleeps, catnapping and waking up every now and then, making sure everything is okay between Mother and baby. Jim says, "Yes, you need some rest, sleep now" He sighed, turning looked out the window,

now the sun is shining bright looking over the fields of corn and cotton. "Time to hitch up the mules and go to work," he says to himself as he walks out the room. Jim, the new father plows the fields.

"Giddy up mule, go mule," as the plow cuts into the ground, turning over the dirt. He hears a horse galloping in his direction, he looks up, it's his boss, Mister Hinton.

Jim: "Good morning, Sir," he says, "How you feel this morning, Sir".

Hinton: "Much obliged, boy." How come you ain't out he plowing this land this morning.

Jim: I was up all night; my wife had a baby —an eight-pound baby girl.

Hinton: Well nigger you shoulda had a boy, we need more nigga boys than gals, next time you better have a boy or I'll have your woman myself and give her a fine half breed boy ya hear."

Hinton laughs and turns his horse to ride away. "Hey boy, I bet your old gal is a good lay. Soon as she gets well, I'll pay a visit." Hinton laughs again, turns away and rides off. Jim says to himself "over my dead body, ain't no goddamn peckerwood gonna screw my wife, I'll kill that son-of-a-bitch." Jim goes to the water trough where the mule is drinking, he washes his face, relaxes and cool off. He takes a deep breath, sits for a moment and looks at the pocket watch his father gave him. "Uh, lunch time." He unhitches the mules to feed them and takes them to a shade tree nearby. He ties them up while they eat. Jim stops by the well, pumps some water and puts his lips to the lip of the pump. He takes a drink and spit part of it out, wrenches his mouth and drinks.

Jim is 26 years old, a big strapping man at 6'3". He has brown muscular skin, a hard body and cold black eyes. He inherited his semi-straight hair from his great grandfather who was part Cherokee Indian. He walks to the porch, pats his dog Root, and smiles to himself. He washes his hands in a tub of water drawn from the well. He dries his hands, walks to the bedroom over to the bed and kisses his wife on the forehead. He picks up the baby and kisses her on the jaw. Tears came to his eyes at that moment, he had a flash that they had to leave Mississippi. He saw his little girl making it big as a singer in the big city. As he day dreamed, he was jolted back to reality by his wife calling him, "Jim, Jim." He looked at his wife and a tear rolled down his eyes.

Jim: "Yes, Jewel."

Jewel: "Don't hold her so tight you'll squeeze her to death."

| Jim: | "Oh baby girl I am sorry, I am just so happy to be a father, my little queen, my little princess, she gonna make us all proud one day." |
| Jewel: | "Oh Jim stop daydreaming, go eat your lunch. There's hot biscuits, black eyed peas and okra, if you want it." |

Jim walks back to the kitchen and looks to the left by the door, he sees a baby cradle with a rocker on both sides. "Where'd this come from?" Jewel replies, "Old man Hinton sent it for the baby by his Uncle Tom house nigger Joe."

Jim mutters under his breath, "That mutherfucker, I'll kill him. We got to get away from here." Jim sits down to eat. As he was eating, he was thinking of how he was going to get his family out of Mississippi. He thought of his friend Jessie who helped people get to Chicago. For a price he would drive to Jackson. For a price they could catch the train North. Next Sunday he'd talk to Jessie at church. He knows he would have to sneak out late at night, walk about two miles through the fields to meet Jessie at a certain point or leave from Church on a Sunday. Then he'll drive about five hours to Jackson to the train that takes them to Chicago. Everybody knew that up North they were hiring everybody to work at the war plant and the slaughterhouse. All you had to say that you were leaving to fight for your country, and you wouldn't have no problem with the law when on the train. After all, World War II had started in Germany, France and England. Before he knew it, he was through eating, heard the midwife call him, "Jim, Jim", it's 1:00, time to go back to work." Jim drank his last drop of milk, cleaned off his plate and put them in the dish tub with the rest of the dishes to be washed for supper. As he walked past the bedroom door, as saw that his wife Jewel was asleep with the baby on her stomach. Her eyes looked up at him and smiled with her big ole pretty eyes. He blew her a kiss, walked out the door to hitch up the mules.

"Damn this sun is hot, said Jim. I'm tired of this shit, kissing peckerwoods asses no sir, yes, sir, no ma'am, yes ma'am. Me and my family are getting out of here as soon as I can." Jim didn't have much money saved, only about $10.00 just enough to pay for the trip to Jackson. He hitched up the mules and went back to the fields. At six p.m. he took the mules to the barn to feed and give them water and brush them down He went home to wash up and eat dinner: black eyed peas, fatback greens, corn bread and lemonade. The old RCA radio was playing on the kitchen shelf. He heard Gabriel Heather, the announcer, talking something of the war in Germany overseas. Jim is not concerned about the war, he's only thinking of his wife and daughter, how he's gonna get the hell out of Mississippi.

He goes outside, rolls up a Prince Albert cigarette, sits down and rubs his dog's head. Old Root, he calls him. He hears the sound of the critters and bullfrogs down by the creek. He looks up and sees a falling star and makes a wish. "God how can I get out of here?", he thinks. Always say when you make a wish on a falling star it will come true. He takes his last drag off his cigarette, put it out with his right foot, rubs his dog's head once again and walks into the house.

Jim undresses in the corner of the bedroom and falls asleep in the room next to his wife and baby. As he dozes off to asleep, he sees the midwife holding the baby and rocking the rocking chair. Knew the next day was Sunday and he would see Jesse and they would discuss how to get him and his family out of Mississippi.

Jim is dreaming about when he first started working for Mr. Hinton. As Jim is brushing down the mules in the barn, Old Man Hinton comes in, a real redneck. He drank a lot so he was red faced, about six feet tall, pot gut, and he held chewing tobacco in his right jaw. "Hey boy, shouts Old Man Hinton, How's them fields coming along. Ya know we planting that tobacco soon. I want them fields ready by next weekend to seed." Standing with his whip in his hand, his gun on his side one could tell the fear in Old Man Hinton's eyes. He was afraid of Jim, but he talked big with his gun on his side, but always stayed six or seven feet away from Jim. When he had his boys with him, he would get right up in Jim's face. As Old Man Hinton talked, his heart starts to pound and his mind went back when he first started working for Old Man Hinton. The year he didn't make his quota in the fields. It was his first time working by himself.

Old Man Hinton and his Boys John Lewis and V.J. tied him up in the barn and Old Man Hinton took the whip to him. Took three months to heal. Hadn't been for Jewel and her knowledge of herbs he would have died. She used slippery elm and comfrey to heal the sores on his back and legs. The crack of the whip brought Jim's thoughts back to the voice of Mr. Hinton. "Ya hear me nigga, I said by next week," as he cracked the whip again. "Yessah Boss, they be ready by next weekend," he said under his breath. "Yessah, next weekend."

It was 5:00 a.m. Sunday morning and the rooster crowed. Half walking up from slumber, Jim hears his daughter crying, Jewel is awake and the midwife asleep in the rocking chair. Jim drags himself up and rubs his eyes. He walks over to the bed, picks up his daughter and comforts her with his Southern charm, "It's alright, my little Princess." He goes to the kitchen and holding the baby in one arm he kindles a fire in the old wood stove and puts the iron eye over the flame. He pours some water in a little pan, puts in the glass baby bottle and waits for the bottle to warm up. He tests the bottle after about five minutes, making sure that it is not too hot, testing it on his arm, then gives it to the baby. She takes the nipple of the bottle and relaxes in his arm. He lays on the bed with the baby carefully so as not to crush her. He puts her half arm length away besides the cotton pillow his wife made.

At about 9:00 a.m. he is shaken gently by the midwife to get up, half awake he smells the bacon and coffee. The midwife takes the baby. He goes to the tub and washes his hands and face and sits down to eat breakfast. Afterward, his wife comes to the table. "Good morning", Jim says. "Good morning, Jim" as she serves his breakfast which consists of bacon, eggs, grits and Wonder bread. She sees a solemn look on Jim's face and says "What's wrong, Daddy, look like you just lost your best friend." "Nothing baby, just thinking to myself." He is wondering how they are going to leave. "'Bout what." "Going to church," he replies. Jim looks at his watch, it's 9:00 o'clock straight up (thinks to himself got two hours to get to church). It's 11:00 a.m., "You going to church with me this morning." "No Jim, I'm gonna wait while until I'm well. But why don't you go and let everybody know I am alright. All right, honey. I'll go and give them the good news about my precious little Princess."

Jim finishes his breakfast and leaves the house to go to the barn. He puts the saddle on the mule and checks the mule's shoes to make sure he's okay. He mounts the mule and starts his journey to church. He guides the mule out of the gate towards the road passing the fields of cotton, corn, and tobacco. He thinks about how he would approach Jesse about leaving, thought to himself didn't want to tell Jewel about leaving because women talk too much. Didn't want to take the chance for the boss to find out about them leaving here.

Jim arrives at church and greets his friends, John, James, Huck, relatives and a host of friends. He tells the Pastor about his new baby. The Pastor announces the arrival of the baby to the church and everybody cheers for him. The church sermon by Rev. Carlise Jones went well. "When my time is over I will fly away, Jim says to himself. I ain't ready to fly away. I want to ride out of this town forever." Church is over. After all shouting and dancing, dancing hand clapping, people exchanging hugs, saying goodbyes until next Sunday, or whenever.

Rev. Jones stood by the door and shook everybody's hand, kissing all the women on the jaw and shaking hands with all the men. The preacher had an old '36 Ford Coupe, six years old. After all this was 1942, didn't too many Negros own cars back then. But all the people in the church pitched in together and bought Rev, a car so he could make his visits and sneak previews, if you know what I mean. He and the Deacon's wife had it going on. The rumor was he was caught with Rev. Miley's wife by one of the young girls. She told him unless he did to her she would tell. The word is he's going with both of them but people lie all the time when it comes to preachers.

Jim approaches Jesse about getting his family out of Mississippi. Jesse sort of look at him and "Jim said "Shoestring." Jesse looked him dead in his eyes and showed a big wide grin. "Well okay then, let's go down by the big tree and talk. *(Shoestring is the secret word used to let people know that certain people can help them leave the South like on a wing and a prayer. But if the wrong person uses it, trying to get information they would wind up dead — found in the river. So people know not to use that term loosely.)* Jim and Jesse walk down by the big oak tree. Jesse told Jim that it would be $25.00; $10.00 each for him and his wife and $5.00 for the baby. Jesse told Jim to bring his wife and child next Sunday, if he had the money. Jim told him he only had $10.00 saved. But Old Man Hinton was going to pay him for the fields next weeks end $40.00 for three months plowing.

'Jim thought about the big, gold and jeweled pocket watch his father gave him. It was worth $400.00 he thought. He showed the watch to Jesse who looked at it and he knew it was worth at least $700.00 gold and all.

Jesse told him if you don't get the money, I'll give you $300.00 for that watch. "I don't know about that, my father gave me this watch. Been in the family for over 100 years." Jesse, yes, I know (saying to himself) boy I could make $400.00 profit off that watch. "This is what I want you to do. When you take the corn to town next week for your boss Old Man Hinton, bring clothes for you, your wife and your baby leave them in the church basement. I medium cured smoked ham for your food, canned peaches, string beans you know they don't spoil too fast. You and your wife can eat a jar of string beans and a jar of peaches a day and canned pet milk for the baby about 10 cans put some well water in three or four gallon jugs and be sure to boil it before you bottle it. Cured smoked ham don't spoil." Jim says, "Okay, I got everything you said." Jesse gives him a note detailing all that he needs. Jim puts the note in his pocket, thanks Jessie and they walk back to the church. Jim mounts his mule and starts home. He gets in a wagon with his family and heads home. They pass the corn, tobacco and cotton as they approach the barn. Mr. Hinton is mounting his horse.

Mr. Hinton shouts, "hey boy". "Morning boss." Mr. Hinton asks, "You been to church boy." Jim replies, "Yessa Boss, I went to church." Mr. Hinton tells him, "I went to see your baby gal too bad she ain't a boy. We silo' could use some more nigga boys around here. Yo' wife look mighty fine, yes yes, mighty fine old gal. Cain't wait to see what she like in bed." Jim uses all his might to hold back his temper. His heart is beating profoundly, sweating he took about ten deep breaths and slid down to the barn floor. Old Man Hinton rode off on his horse saying, "Yes, cain't wait to see what it's like to get her in bed." Jim knowing and hoping this is his last week here, he decided right then and there that he would have to prepare everything right away to leave before he got hung from the highest tree. He slowly pulled himself up from the floor with the help of a plank nailed to the mule stall. His heart is beating, he is sweating and tears fall from his eyes. He stood up as Old Man Hinton rode away in the distance, alongside his wife and boys John Lewis and V.J. one on each side of his wife. Going to evening service about 5 miles in the opposite direction of his church.

Jim went home to the row of shotgun houses, each neatly side by side like slave quarters. Drying the tears from his eyes and breathing hard he feels a sharp pain his chest. He stopped by a tree, sat down and took a long deep breath, kept taking short deep breaths. He dozed off for about thirty minutes. He woke up dreaming about up North, about what he heard, fancy clubs, pretty cars, dancing halls, lots of money, good jobs, and good food. He felt good knowing he was going to finally get up North.

He had a sister in Chicago who lived on Warren Boulevard and Western Avenue. Her name is Hannah. She had a big house and good job. Hannah wrote him about two years ago and asked him if he wanted to come live with her in Chicago, but he refused. He just got married, just landed this job here with Mr. Hinton, $40.00 every three months, room and board.

Jim made more money from Mr. Hinton than lie ever made in his life. Where he came from in Rome, Georgia he was lucky to make $10.00 in three months. Working from boss to boss, plantation to plantation, eating up his salary and sleeping wherever he could. If he knew what he knew now, he would have left 'cause that ass whipping from Mr. Hinton wasn't no joke. Just because he didn't make his quota plowing that first year. Not letting himself get upset he pulls himself up and starts walking home almost running. He got another sharp pain in his chest, took a deep breath and kept walking until he reached the front door. Told his wife about the pain, but not about the conversation with Mr. Hinton until he had fixed some Hawthorn Berry tea for his chest pain. Jewel told him Mr. Hinton came to the house making lewd remarks to her and what he wanted to do to her. Jim didn't let himself get mad, 'cause he knew he would get sick. He just sipped his tea and listened to her and said, "Don't worry baby, everything will be alright."

Jennie, the midwife, comes in. Sort of a strong woman with strong African features. Her daughter Joan was mulatto, very pretty about 18 years old. Joan worked in the big house for the boss — one of his women, she got everything she needed him from. Jennie says hi to Jim. "Hi, Jennie, Jim says, just fine." Joan looks at Jim with lust in her eyes and looks him up and down like she wanted to eat him up. Jim always ignored her. Jim in a sorta dry voice, says "Hi, Joan." "Hi, Jim." Jim knew she couldn't be trusted, less he said around her the better off he would be. She had already got one guy killed. She overheard him talking about he was going to leave and not pay Mr. Hinton. They hung him for all could see how white folks feel about niggers in Mississippi, reinforcing their ideas.

Jim told his wife about the plan. What he didn't know was that, Joan was listening from behind the door and peeping through the keyhole. Joan sneaked out and went back to the big house. She didn't tell Mr. Hinton but she told the house nigger Joe who told Mr. Hinton when he returned.

Meanwhile, Jim got all the stuff he needed for the church. He decided he better do it today while Mr. Hinton was gone to church and visiting his family. He packed all the stuff he needed, while his wife boiled the well water for the gallon jugs. He brought the mule and wagon 'round back of the house. By that time, his wife

15

had gotten the water together so he loaded everything and took it to the church. He came back and unhitched the mule and wagon and waited for the next day to go plow the fields.

Jim worked from Monday to Friday. Saturday he got all the fields plowed and finished the seeding. Mr. Hinton stopped by Saturday evening to pay Jim his $40.00. Jim hears a knock at the door, opens it and in stepped Mr. Hinton and his two boys. He gets up in Jim's face and gives him a long hard look. "Boy, here's your pay, don't spend it all in one place." (not mentioning to Jim that he knew his escape plan). He laughed, walked out and gave a loud shout. "Boy, you niggers are something else, got all these fine brown women, better be careful next time your baby might be white. Ha, ha, ha, ha, ha, ha, ha, ha, ha, ha, ha." Jim looks at the back of Mr. Hinton's head as walked out slamming the door. Jim thinks about tomorrow and getting the hell out of there. The echo of Old Man Hinton's laugher filled the room.

Jim, l¯ris wife and baby get ready for bed. Jim's dog starts howling like never before, tossing and turning all night. About 12:30 a.m., Jim gets up and goes out the door to calm down his old dog Root. As he pats and rubs old Root, he assures him that things would be just fine. He'll come back and get him or have someone to bring him up North. Root calmed down and whines a bit, Jim hugs and pets him and rubs him down. Then he gives Root some leftover food and water.

Jim goes to the pump and knows the squeaking pump will wake up the neighbors. He washed his hands with soap and water, dried them on his clothes, and pulled out the Prince Albert can of tobacco. He rolled himself up a cigarette and looked up at the clear moon lit sky. He sees another falling star and makes a wish hoping that tonight will be his last night here in this town. He takes his last drag off his cigarette and thumped it out onto the cotton field. It flickers from one stalk to another and lands on the ground and burns out. He turns to go back into the house and rubs his dog's head as he passes through the door.

At 5:00 o'clock a.m. on Sunday morning, the rooster crows. It seemed like the longest night of Jim's life. He couldn't sleep a wink all night and just stared at the ceiling. His wife and baby slept like a log. He just lay there until about 7:30 a.m. when the midwife knocked on the door to tell him that breakfast of hot biscuits, rice and gravy, hamburger meatballs, syrup and cold buttermilk was almost ready. Jim dragged himself out of bed and washed up his face and hands. He sits down to eat the breakfast which by now is ready. Jennie comes and sits down with her plate and says she's going to church today with him and his wife. He looks at her and says you want to go to church with us. She says yes, then the word shoestring.

He smiled. Jennie pulls out a roll of money about $3,000 she'd had been saving over 20 years. "I want to leave with you and Jewel. This is enough money for us to live on for a year or more, pay rent, buy food, clothes until we gets jobs. I'm not taking my daughter, she's too close to Old Man Hinton. I don't trust her at all, can I go with ya'll." "Yes, by all means," says Jim. Jewel comes into the kitchen holding the baby and says, "Good morning, ya'll". "Good morning, honey," replies Jim. "Mornin' Jewel, I'll take the baby," says Jennie. Jewel washes her face and hands and dries them off with a towel hanging on a nail by the door. The three of them talked about the plan and they all agree to leave together.

There was a knock at the door. It was Joan, Jennie's daughter. They all looked at each other sort of puzzled by her early appearance. "Morning ya'll," says Joan. Everyone replies, "Morning June." "What brings you down here so early?" June replies, "Oh, Jim I was just thinking about the baby, want to see her." Jim asks, "What was you thinking?" "Oh, nothing really just wanted to see the baby." Okay, she right here, your mother is holding her in the bedroom. Joan walks to the bedroom. Speaks to her mother and takes the baby from her mother. She holds the baby close, talks to her and rocks her. She then brings her back to the kitchen, sits down and says "Are you going to church?" Jewel replies, "Yes, we are going to church, your mother is going with us today." Joan looked stunned. Giving the baby to Jewel she goes into the bedroom where her mother was and begs her not to go to church today. Jennie ignored her so Joan left in a huff.

Sometime later, Jim, Jewel, Jennie and the baby ready to leave for church. Jim hitches the mule to the wagon. He puts blankets on the seats and quilts in the back of the wagon to make traveling more comfortable for the ride to church. They all board the wagon, Jim and Jewel riding up front and Jennie holding Princess in back. Jennie looked over the corn, tobacco and cotton fields knowing deep in her heart that she won't be coining back to this town. She's been waiting all her life to leave but she didn't have the courage and was afraid to leave. She sings a lullaby to the baby humming a song and saying out loud, "Thank you Jesus."

They arrive at church and Jim scans the church about 50 yards down the road. There are many buggies, mules and drawn wagons lined up the side and around and in front of the church. Jim finds a spot across the road in front of the church. He helps Jewel from the wagon and Jennie hands the baby to Jewel. She then climbs from the back of the wagon. Jim tells Jewel and Jennie to take the baby and go into the church.

People are mingling in front of the church, hugging, talking, joking and shaking hands. From the corner of his right eye, Jim sees Jesse approaching. Jesse saunters up to Jesse. He looks around to make sure their conversation nobody is listening and he whispers, "Hi, Jim." "Hey, Jessie. How's it going, everything ready?" "Like clockwork," Jesse whispers back. "Okay, my friend. What about my supplies that I put in the church basement?" "I checked them, they are fine. I fixed and put you your food and stuff in a double cardboard box, knives, forks, spoons, some small towels that I didn't need. By the way, what about the watch?" Jim has decided to keep his father's watch, "What about it?" "You still want to sell it for $350.00." "No, Jesse. I got lucky. I got all the money for the trip." "Okay, Jesse I understand." "Me and my wife is taking Jennie our midwife with us." "Okay that will be $35.00 for you, Jewel, Jennie and the baby. All your things are in the trunk of my car."

Reverend Carlise Jones was preaching his sermon, "You can't take it with you." As Jim and Jesse walk into the church. Jesse sits up front; Jim sits with his wife, baby and Jennie. Reverend Jones preaches, "You can't take it with you, yeah. You can have a fine car, a big house, fine clothes, all the money and gold, but one thing I know, aha, you can't take it with you. So you better get right with God, if you don't want to burn in hell, cause living in sin and die in sin. God won't never bother your soul again, he'll let Satan win. You are going straight to hell, so you better get right with God, aha, yeah. I say ya better get right with the Lord, get him in your heart, get him in your soul, cause he'll `sho make you feel whole ..."

Mr. Hinton and his sons saddle up to go to church. He had heard of Jim's plans to escape to the North. In the meantime, as Old Man Hinton and his boys are riding past the fields of corn, tobacco and cotton, he happens to looks over his shoulder about a mile in the opposite direction and sees a fire spreading and heading for his home. He tells his boys and they turn around and gallop their horses pass their house taking blankets and water in a wagon. They try to stop the fire, throwing water and beating the fire with blankets. With all the sharecroppers hands it takes them almost 3 hours to contain the fire.

Jesse tells Jim that it's best they leave now while the church is still full, not knowing that Mr. Hinton had a fire near his house which saved their lives. Jim fetches Jewel and Jennie and they pile up in Jesse's car; the women in the back and the men in front. The car pulls off by the jerking of the gears.

Jesse had a '34 Ford Coupe, four door sedan he had won in a crap game, title and all. Jesse was sporting a zoot suit he was a sharp dresser. In the '40's, there were people who were sharecroppers who worked the land and couldn't get jobs. They were indentured servants under the thumb of the white man. They didn't have a choice.

They were like slaves, working the land for a living, never getting ahead, the only way out was to escape to the North or die.

From a life of poverty, physical abuse, mayhem and possible death by hanging from the highest tree. It was very common for Negros to be hung by the neck until dead, tarred and feathered. Castration was very common. To avoid the possibility of these terrible things Jim didn't have a chance, no more than a snowball in hell. If he showed even an inkling of defiance toward Mr. Hinton about what he had said about his pretty brown skinned wife he could be killed.

Jewel was a sight for sore eyes, smooth dark skin like silk, she was part Chactow and African. She had a black hourglass figure, firm breasts, beautiful strong legs, an oval face, beautiful dreamy eyes and a race horse placed-just-right rump. The riding kind that would make any man's eyes pop out. Just use your imagination. She was five feet, six and one half inches tall. For a woman in those days a real pony, as they say.

Jewel could feel freedom ring and tears came to her eyes. She gently wiped her eyes and laughed with joy. Everyone was silent until they were on the highway going north to Jacksonville, Mississippi. Jim was sitting in front like a huge African king, listening to the hum of the tires gripping the hot highway beneath them. The hot evening wind was hitting him in the face and he let out a loud scream, "Free at last, free at last."

The sign read 100 miles from Jacksonville, Mississippi which was about two and one-half hours to go. They were scheduled to leave by bus to Biloxi, Mississippi and then catch a train to Chicago. The highway was hot and you could see for miles around. The sun was glaring, the heat hot on the highway and hot air blowing through all the open windows. Jennie starts to sing, "Thank you Lord for bringing us out that hell hole, cause I am on the battlefield for my Lord."

Jesse sees a sign which alerts him that the next gas station is 50 miles down the road. He tells Jim he has to stop for gas, about two miles up the road. They see a Texaco station and Jesse pulls into the station. He buys $1.50 worth of gas and checks the oil and water. The price is $.20 per gallon of gas. He gets extra gas in a gas can in case they run short to Jacksonville. The station owner asks where they are going and Jesse tells him they are going to a funeral in Jacksonville, his aunt has died. After a two and one half hour drive, they arrive in Jacksonville. They spend the night at a boarding house (safe house). Jesse knew the owner. Everything was planned out: $35.00 for Jim, Jewel, Jennie and the baby. The owner had the tickets ready. Jim paid for the tickets. $5.00 each for the grownups, the baby rides free on the train. The train leaves at 6:00 a.m. Everybody was up and ready at 4:30 a.m., thirty minute ride to the train. They arrived at the station an hour early so they could get their seats and find the right car: (F10) through (G10) Colored Only, 10 cars for whites, 10 cars for colored people.

Jesse spoke to Jim and told him what to say to the Conductor. "If he asks you where you are going, tell him to the North to join the Army to fight for our country and tell him it's great to be an American," he said with a big wide grin on his face. The conductor looks at him, shakes his head and says dumb nigger to himself. You ain't got no country and shakes his head. Jim smiles, "Yes sir boss." The Conductor thinks, you black ass nigger is the first on the front line, don't you know we put all the niggers on the front line, so our boys (white boys) can come back home. We trying to kill all off ya'll, any God bless you. Give me them tickets, I show ya'll yo' seats. As they walked through the train cars, Jim was amazed to see all these colored folks getting away from the South. They finally found their seats, they had a private room with closed doors in the Coach section for an extra few dollars. Jim sat by the window and his wife and Jennie sat across from him, facing him. He had the baby in a basket next to him, holding the basket with his right hand.

The train rumbled along the tracks and made a whistling sound smoke blowing from the engine. As the train pulled out the station, Jim looked out the window at the white people standing, laughing and talking among themselves. The train picked up speed and he could see all the Blacks huddled in a corner of the station looking like a flash of mannequins. Then the countryside began to appear, cow and horses grazing in the fields, cotton fields and tobacco fields rushing by as the train roared by in a big flash.

Jim asked Jewel for the lunch box, she said it was in the overhead compartment. He stood up, reached over her head and pulled the basket and box containing the cold chicken, bread, lemonade, sweet potato pie, can of peaches and string beans. A day and a half from Jackson to Chicago.

Jim takes some pieces of chicken leg and thigh offers some to Jewel and Jennie. Both decline. They weren't hungry yet. They were too thrilled to be leaving the South to be hungry. They cried sobbing to themselves. "Thank you Jesus, thank you Jesus." The baby wakes up and Jewell takes her and begins to breastfeed her. Meanwhile, Jim eats chicken, drinks some lemonade and eats a piece of potato pie. Jennie and Jim fall asleep. When Jewel finishes feeding the baby, she places her in the basket and falls asleep. Night falls and everyone is still asleep.

Back at the Hilton Plantation, Old Man Hinton is furious because Jim left and the fields weren't finished.

He lined up all the plantation workers in the front of their homes early Monday morning. His head house nigger torn Joe was there and told Mr. Hinton in front of everyone what Joan had told him. Old Man Hinton standing, shaking with whip in hand, the other hand on his gun threatening to everyone to whip or shoot them, if they didn't tell him about Jim, his wife and Jennie escaping from his plantation to go up North. Only Jennie's daughter knew because by accident she overheard them talking about the plan.

Old Man Hinton was so furious he made everyone work the fields from 6:00 a.m. until 7:00 p.m. for a whole month. He even overworked the horses. He whipped two of his field hands, hung one to make an example for the other field hands to see. He was really mad because he wanted Jim's wife for himself. She was a beauty to behold, the kind of beauty a man could not forget once he laid his eyes on her. Mr. Hinton's friend from another plantation sold her and her mother to him.

Jewel's mother had died from pneumonia and she was raised by other field hands. Hinton never noticed her until after Jim married her Old Man Hinton would dream about her at night, have wet dreams about her. He was heartbroken and would wake up in a cold sweat at night. He planned to hire bounty hunters in Chicago to bring them back. After all Jim owed him money for the winter crops. When Old Man Hinton went back to the big house, all the field hands jumped for joy because Jim and his family escaped from the demonic forces of the plantation forever. Praise God.

After riding the train for 14 hours, Jim woke up at about 4:00 a.m. as the train came to a halt and jerked to a station in Rome near Memphis, Tennessee. He heardpeople talking and he peered through the shade to see the Conductor talking to two men dressed in suits. They were looking at the train. The Conductor shook his head as if to soothe the men. It started to rain and the train started to move slowly. The Conductor said "All aboard" and the train started to move really fast. About thirty minutes later, Jim heard a tap on the door. It was the Conductor beckoning Jim to come outside. He said, "Those men were bounty hunters looking for you and your family. The only reason I didn't give them up is because of your little baby girl, I have one myself. Although I am not fond of colored people, I can't see breaking up a family. But for my help I'll charge you $5.00 and you won't have any more problems with them at all, you'll arrive safe in Chicago."

Jim tells him to wait a minute and he returns to the inside coach. He tells Jennie what he learned and she gives him 5 one dollar bills. Jim gives it to the Conductor saying, "This is half of what we got to make it to Chicago."

The Conductor says, "Okay, between you and me keep your mouth closed, I could lose my job for helping a ni—a colored person. Go on back it's okay I am conducting this train to Chicago, you are safe for now." Jim thanked him and went back to his seat and fell asleep.

In the other cars, the colored people were talking in low voices, keeping their children quiet and trying their best not to make any noise because they know they could be put off the train in the middle of nowhere. It happens quite often to colored people, if the Conductor doesn't like you. As the train rumbled down the tracks the Conductor was summoned by the engineer. The train slowed up coming around the bend. A tree had fallen over the tracks. The Conductor came to the colored section of the train and summoned about 20 men (boys as they called them) to saw the tree and remove it from the tracks. A saw was brought out from the baggage car. The colored boys took turns sawing the tree while the whites looked on. One white boy says to his mother, "What are those niggers doing." She says, "Michael, don't use that word. Those are colored boys not niggers." "My Dad says...," the mother cut him off saying, I don't care what your Dad says, don't use that word around me." All the other white people in the car gave her a long hard look. One white woman says to another, "Nigger lover." They all laughed. The tree was a big pine tree and had fallen across the tracks. As the colored boys sawed the pine tree they sang the song, "Tell ole Pharaoh to let my people go." The rhythm of the saw kept up with the song they were singing. As each piece was cut it was tossed down the canyon adjacent to the tracks.

Jewel and Jennie woke up and looked out the train window wondering what happened. The train had stopped and they heard a lot of commotion, talking, and noise. Jewel worried about Jim so she set out to find out what happened, what was going on. As she opened the door to the sleeper a woman told her the problem. She went back and sat down, told Jennie and they waited for Jim to return. After three hours, Jim returned jingling 50 cents in dimes and nickels for the work he had done. Jim and Jewel talked a while about Old Man Hinton, then they fell asleep as the train roared throughout the night smoke bellowing from the engine.

About 7:30 a.m. Little Princess starts to fret, Jewel wakes up and picks Princess up. She reaches in her bag and gets a diaper. Then she goes to the restroom inside the berth which is so small only one person can enter. She found out when she turned the water on it was hot and cold, she had read about it in an old Life magazine years ago. There was an article on trains, all about trains. She turned on the water and cleaned the baby, flushed the toilet, washed one hand then the other, dried one then the other, all while holding Princess. Jewel returned to her seat, opened up the bag and took out a towel, which she laid on her chest. She then breast fed Princess and when she fell asleep she put her back in her basket covered her well with the blanket. Jewel relaxes back in her seat and fell asleep. Jim wakes up as Jewel is falling into a deep sleep and asks if she is okay. Jewel replies, "yes" and starts to snore in a low murmur. Jim squeezes into the bathroom, he knew about trains because he read the article with Jewel. Jim's six foot, four and one-half inch frame could just get into the restroom, but he managed to take care of his business. Jim emerges from the bathroom after cleaning himself and washing his hands, relaxes back in his seat and falls asleep.

The train came to a jerking halt and everybody woke up. Jim wonders where they are and peers out of the window. The sign over the station reads "St Louis, Missouri." Jeanie wakes up and goes into the bathroom, washes up and asks Jim to take down the food. She eats some chicken, peaches, cornbread and then drinks a glass of water. She told Jewel that she was going to take a walk through the train, and to watch her purse because all the money was in the purse.

Jeanie opens the door, leaves the berth and walks up the aisle looking at the different people, different dress. Up the aisles on the left she sees one of her old flames she hadn't seen in about five years. She remembers about all the good times she had with him. He left Mr. Hinton's place to go to another plantation because Mr. Hinton's friend was short of help. As their eyes met a big smile came upon his face. "Lord, Lord, looka here, girl, I've been thinking and thinking about you, wondering if I would ever see you again." James was by himself. He had escaped from Ole Mr. Hinton's friend's plantation and hid out for two weeks in the woods until he contacted the right people. He and Jim had worked together for about two years before he left the plantation. They talked about the old times and the future. Jennie was a short, plump woman in her mid-forties with smooth black skin. Her hair was nicely worn in braids or plaits, one on each side of her head. James was in his early '40s, tall at six feet, two and one-half inches, 190 pounds, muscular, with brown skin and whe wore his short curly hair close to his head. He had a full mouth of teeth and was neatly dressed. James was on his way to Chicago to live with his brother on Washington Boulevard around the corner from Warren Boulevard, the same area where Jim and Jewel would be living.

The passengers were getting off the train and the shout of the Conductor got their attention, "All aboard, next stop Springfield, Illinois, then Chicago." Jennie told James to come with her to see Jim and Jewel and their new baby. She took him by the hand and lead him down the aisle then through the three coach cars. They arrived and tapped at the berth's door. Jim called out "Who is it?" and Jennie replied, "It's Jennie, Jim open the door, surprise!" Jim's eyes got big with a big wide grin on his face, "James, man what a surprise, where you been, I missed you a lot." "Me too, man", James replies. "Where you going, man?" "Chicago, man," they say to each other.

Jim tells James to sit down and says, "You hungry, we got some hot lemonade, water, chicken, peaches, string beans and cornbread." James says, "Yeah man, I ain't ate in two days. I could use some food." James takes the food and eats slowly and earnestly. He finishes eating while Jewel and Jennie are talking to Jim. Jim looks at his big gold watch, "We be in Chicago in two hours. Thank God, thank you Jesus." The others say, "Amen, thank you Jesus." Two hours pass while they chit chat about old times and this and that. The Conductor taps on the door saying, "Get your stuff ready, we'll be pulling into the station in 20 minutes." Everybody gathers their things and Jim packs up the remaining food. James leaves and comes back with his bags. At Union Station, everybody gets off the train. Jim carries the bags and Jewel carries the baby. Jennie's arm is wrapped in James and James is looking down at her, each smiling and happy as they walked.

Jim's sister Hannah was standing by the baggage with her boyfriend, soon to be husband. Hannah saw Jim and Jewel with the baby. Hannah gave Jim a big hug and hugs Jewel. She then takes the baby and tells them how beautiful the baby is. Jim introduces Jennie and James. Hannah knew that Jennie was coming with them. She thought James was excess baggage until she saw his brother approaching. James called out to his brother Marvin. James hugged his brother and told him how glad he was to see him.

Hannah had a "39 Ford four door coupe and Marvin had a '36 Ford Coupe. They all got into the big car with Hannah and her boyfriend. They exchanged addressed and phone numbers and James left with his brother.

FIRST DAY IN CHICAGO

Everybody arrived at their respective houses. Jim takes in the bags, Jewel carries Princess and Jennie carries her own bags. Jim and Jewel had their own room and Jennie hers. Jim and Jewel's room was adjacent to the kitchen and Jeannie's was off from theirs. Hannah had a large bedroom next to the dining room. The kitchen was small to medium sized enough for three people. There was no fence in the backyard off the kitchen.

Jim went into the bathroom and ran some water in the tub. He soaked in the tub for a long time, closed his eyes, laid back in the tub and reminisced on his trip, his family and Mr. Hinton. He laughed to himself, his trip flashed through his mind and he laughed again. He bathed himself real good, rinsed off with the shower hose in hand and then dried himself off. He then shaved, brushed his teeth, put on his pajamas, combed his hair and cleaned out the bathtub. He went to his bedroom, got on his knees and thanked God in the name of Jesus. He knew in his mind all colored people had a strong belief in God and Jesus Christ.

Jewel went into the bathroom and washed herself Meanwhile Jim crawled in bed with the baby Princess, moved her arms lengthwise so he wouldn't crush her and fell asleep. Jewel returns to see that Jim and Princess are fast asleep. Jemiie goes to the bathroom and asks Jewel how everything works. Jewel tells and demonstrates everything to her from the toilet to the wash basin. Jewel returns to bed, stretched out and cuddles Princess in her arms and falls asleep.

The next day everybody is up at 8:00 a.m. dressed and sitting at the table for breakfast. They have a delicious breakfast of hot biscuits, meatballs, gravy, syrup, butter and buttermilk. Hannah inquires, "Ya'll enjoy your trip up here." Jim replied, "Yes, very good trip. Couple of minor problems, but the good Lord took care of everything. Yes he sho' did." He laughed and smiled, ha, ha, ha. Jewel chimed in, "We had a very nice trip." Hannah tells them to make themselves at home and that after a while they will all take a ride around Chicago so that "Ya'll can see the City."

Later everybody piles into Hannah's "39 Ford, Hannah is at the wheel, Jim next to her, Jewel, Princess and Jennie in the back seat. Hannah backs out of the alley, turns left onto Warren Boulevard headed downtown to the Loop. Jim, Jewel and Jennie are amazed at the tall buildings and the people all dressed up in suits and ties. Police are directing traffic. They arrived at Jew Town on Maxwell and Halstead. Hannah tells them about Jew Town and how to get a cheaper price for what you want. If he gives you a lower price you give him a lower price, you keep haggling until you get the price you like. As they walked from stall to stall, Jewel saw a nice gold plated Timex watch with a black leather strap for $2.50. She bargained the salesman down to a price of $1.00. Jim bought a pair of Stacy Adams shoes for $3.00, half of the regular price. Jennie bought a nice top of the line Sears brand summer dress for $4.00 which was regularly priced at $7.00. Hannah bought a pair of reading glasses and they all bought one of Chicago's Jew Town famous Polish sausages followed by a cold Coca Cola. They finished eating as they walked back to the car. They piled into the car again and went to the movies to see a John Dillinger movie *The Lady in Red*. Jim, Jewel and Jennie had never been to the movies before or seen a picture show, although they had read about them in Life magazine. They were fascinated by the buttered popcorn.

After arriving home from the movies, Jim could not stop talking about the movie. He was fascinated that Princess had slept all through the movie, she was such a good baby. They gave her plenty of attention. Everybody gets a good night sleep.

The next day they had the same routine as the day before except that Hannah told Jim about on the job training as a porter janitor. Jim will start Monday downtown at the Tribune Tower with Hannah's boyfriend. He had Friday through Sunday to rest and listen to the radio. Jim was fascinated by the radio, Tom Mix, the Shadow, the Invisible Man, the war programs, etc. The only radio he heard was Mr. Hinton's for a few moments when he went to the big house to get food and supplies for the mule and field when he was plowing.

One day as Jim arrived at work he was awed by a big black limousine which pulled to the curb in front of the Tribune building. As he opened the door, a big man bolted from the car and rushed toward him. Jim hurried and opened the door and the man flipped him a 50 cent piece. Three or four men followed, they were big men with long black overcoats. Two stayed by the long limousine. Jim went back to work happy that the white man gave him a 50 cent piece. He could buy lunch for a whole week and buy some milk for Princess. Jim later learned that the big man was Al Capone.

Jim looked at his pocket watch it was getting close to quitting time, two more hours to go. He just finished his sandwich and Coke. He had a half of floor to finish, pick up trash, dust, sweep and mop the bathroom areas. Jim was a good worker, always very clean and he kept his floors in excellent condition. When it was time to quit work, Jim met Hannah's boyfriend at the time clock. They spoke, punched out and got in Hannah's car which was parked in the back of the Tribune Tower. Hannah's boyfriend Elmo said, "Jim, I checked your work." Jim says, "yeah." "You do very good work, just like a pro", exclaims Elmo. "The boss told me that if you keep up the good work, he'll give you a raise to $50.00 a week." Jim says, "Man, that's $200.00 a month, boy I could buy me a car and soon get me a house for my family, pay Hannah $50.00 a month for rent." Elmo says, "Hold on Jim listen to me. First off you gotta be tested for this job. I mean probation for six months, you gotta understand these white people gonna check you out first. You know if you pan out and be a good nigger then they will keep you. If not, you are going kibosh out. But if you play your cards right, be good, play your cards right, be good, don't miss work, do a good job like you are doing you'll be fine. When they got to 2345 Warren Boulevard where Jim lives, Hannah was waiting at the door to let them in. Elmo had called Hannah to let her know that he was stopping by to spend the night. Jim entered his room in the back near the kitchen. Jewel was set up in bed half sleepy, rubbing her eyes yawning, she says hi to him. "Hi," says Jim "how's the baby, my little Princess?" "She's okay, replies Jewel, she has a little colic. Your sister Hannah made some tea and fed it to the baby with an eye dropper. The tea seemed to calm her and she finally went to sleep. Let me fix you a snack, some cheese and bologna and milk, it'll make you sleep better tonight." "Okay, babe, I'll go wash my hands," says Jim. He goes into the bathroom, uses the bathroom and washes his hands and face and dries them on a towel hanging on a nail. Then he went back to the bedroom. Jewel brought the food to the bed while Jim laid back on the bed for a few seconds, then raised up and took a bite of the meat, cheese and crackers. He took a sip of milk and concentrated on listening to Count Basie on the radio, then Duke Ellington. The jazz music was soothing to his ears, "man" he says to himself, "I am so relaxed" and he dozed off to sleep.

Jewel removed the cheese, bologna and milk from the night stand, took it back to the kitchen and put it in the ice box. Ice at the top, food in the bottom. Then she slipped under the covers, turned out the light and fell asleep next to Jim with the baby in the crib beside the bed.

The next morning at 6:45 a.m. Princess awakes up Jewel with her crying. Jewel stretches, tells the baby' "shhh Daddy is sleeping." She picks up Princess and leans her over her shoulder, put her back and changes her diaper. Jewel walks back to the kitchen, rinsed out the bottle with hot water, poured milk in a pot on the stove. She turned on the gas burner to heat the milk. After about five minutes, she checked the bottle, walking and patting Princess on the back of her shoulder. She checked the milk over her wrist from the bottle, it's okay to give to Princess. She returns to the bedroom and lays Princess on her chest while Princess takes the bottle of milk and she finally goes to sleep.

Jewel returns to the bedroom, lays the baby in her crib and cuddles up to Jim and falls back to sleep dreaming about the difference between the South and the North. Remembering keeping ice in the ground, covered with a heavy quilt, with meat wrapped in brown wax paper to keep from getting wet or too soggy. Vegetables from the garden, taking a bath in a #50 wash tub, no electrical lights, oil lamps (cold oil), wood stove, outside toilet. "Wow, what a difference." She thought here we have an ice box, ice at top, food at bottom, a bath tub, shower and toilet. Jewel was so excited in the difference. She could buy canned vegetables, peas, greens, meat in the can. "Boy, we are living good, she thought, thank you Jesus for all these goodies to eat, a place to stay clean, yes thank you Jesus, amen."

The next day at 8:00 a.m. Jim is awakened by the sound of the alarm clock. He yawns and stretches. The light is shining through the window and he reaches up and pulls back the shade. It is snowing and he stares at the snow. His mind drifts back to Mississippi thinking about the winter time in the South, hitching up the mules to the wagon going to the woods cutting up logs for the wood stove, for Mr. Hinton's house and his house, and the other sharecroppers. His friend Bo who he left behind, his dog he misses a lot wondering what happened to him, he really misses his friend. He snaps to reality when his wife touches him calls him in a sweet voice, "Jim, Jim, get up, wash up, come and eat your breakfast."

Jim snaps back to reality, gets up and goes to the bathroom. He comes out, sits at the table to a plate of grits, bacon, eggs and coffee. His wife sits on his lap, hugs him and gives him a quick kiss saying, "Baby, I am so happy, yes, we can take a bath in a bathtub or shower, you got a ice box." She goes over and opens the door, she opens the cupboard, "we got canned foods and all these goodies, thank you Jesus." Jim says, "yes baby" as he hits her on her fanny, then he came time to eat his breakfast.

1943 — six months later. Princess is playing on the floor with ABC blocks putting them in her mouth, trying to bite them, slobbering at the mouth with one tooth showing. Jewel is playing with her baby. Jewel and Hannah are watching the cars go by in the streets while listening to Arthur Godfrey Hour Variety Show. Jim wakes up and comes into the living room, he surprises Jewel by telling her he passed the probation period, and got a raise up to $200.00 a month.

A year later, Jim and Jewel enrolled their daughter in the first grade at grammar school on Walcott Avenue. Princess is now six and one-half years old. Princess liked school. She already knew her abc's, she was a quick learner, she was always picked for school plays, like Peter Pan, singing in choirs for children, dancing. Jewel would walk Princess to school and pick her up every day.

1953, ten years later, Princess is playing in the streets at age 11, playing hopscotch with her friends. By now, Jim and Jewel have bought a house which has two bedrooms, kitchen, bath, living room, stove, and refrigerator. They even bought a television on time at $3.00 a month. Jim is still working at the Tribune Tower now making $400.00 a month with a retirement plan, life insurance, bank account, and car. Everything was going along fine. Jewel got pregnant with her second child, a girl they named Joan.

When Joan was born, Princess got a little jealous at first. Finally she got used to the new baby and she would go to the new crib, hold her hand and talk and sing to her. At church, little Princess had a strong voice. She sang in the choir and sang lead on all the church songs. She could really rock the house on Sunday.

Willie Johnson aka Slick Willie was a song producer. He heard about Little Princess, and her strong a cappella voice with a ten octave range, she could hold a note for over two minutes, if need be. Slick Willie goes to church and meets Jim and Jewel. He asks them about their daughter's strong voice and was glad to meet them. He explained to them that he was a record producer, it wasn't uncommon in the '40's and '50's to record children on blues songs and rock and rock and gospel songs. Correct me if I'm wrong, there was a young girl in the '50's named Betty Lou Williams, she was a gospel singer. There were lots of black child prodigies in the '30's, '40's and '50's.

Lorenzo was walking in front of Princess' house, she and some friends were playing hopscotch on the sidewalk. Princess looks up and their eyes meet, she fell in a slight trance. He looked awed and says to himself, "Wow, she's pretty, I really like her." Princess was caught for a brief second. She daydreamed pretending she was a leading lady in the movies thinking of him holding her and kissing her like Clark Gable kissing his leading lady. She is jolted back to reality when she hears her mother's voice calling, "Princess, come in girl it's time to eat." Princess picks up her jump rope and tells her friend Connie that she has go to in to eat dinner. She heard her mother ask, "Who was that boy talking to you." Princess replies, "Oh,that was Lorenzo we go to school together." Mother says, "Oh, do he always talk to you?' "No, he never say nothing, just look at me, and smile. That was the first time he ever smiled at me." "Do you like him?" "No, I don't even know him." Princess says to herself if she only knew, I do like him.

Slick Willie and Princess are in the studio. Willie is laying down tracks for a gospel session with Princess. Her parents are there in the studio. Her mother sings in the choir, she is one of the choir directors. Princess sings in the children's choir. As Princess sings her mother coaches her, "Boy, she has a strong voice for a young girl at the age of 13." After the session, Jim and Jewel leave to walk the three blocks home. They leave Princess to do some voiceovers on a couple of songs. Princess had seen movies before when men kiss women. She always wondered how it felt. As Princess sings her song, Slick Willie sidles up to her and puts his arm around her waist, holds her close and tells her how pretty she is and how he is gonna make her a star. She felt his strong body close to hers. She felt warm and tingling in her stomach, that he like her and he would be her secret boyfriend, if she didn't tell anyone. He felt her young body close to his, put his hand under her dress. She was awestruck when he felt her private parts it felt different and good. He kissed her on he cheek. They heard footsteps coming up the stairs. Slick

Willie told Princess to go back into the recording booth and he played the music. She started to sing as her father walked into the room, opening the door to the room. With a cool look on his face not sensing anything out of the ordinary he listened to his daughter sing. He was proud of his daughter. Jim had said from the day she was born, she would become a great singer.

The next day, Lorenzo and Princess meet in school. Lorenzo sees Princess walking down the hallway, he gives her that same look when he saw her on the sidewalk, when she was playing hopscotch. Princess smiled, she was shy. Lorenzo finally tries to talk to Princess, "Say, didn't I see you playing hopscotch on the sidewalk on Warren Boulevard?" Princess, "Oh, yeah I think so." Lorenzo asks if he can walk her home from school. Princess says she doesn't care. Lorenzo says, "okay, see you later."

After school they meet, Lorenzo hurried out of his classroom, almost running. He knew Princess was waiting for him on the side of Walcott Street by the bus stop. He sees her, her head down looking at the ground she was sort of daydreaming. She looked a bit startled, he was so quiet when he approached, she looked up and he said, "Hi," Princess says. Lorenzo, replies, "Hi, you okay." "Yes, why?" "Oh nothing, you looked a bit surprised." "Oh, I was just thinking." "Bout what." "Oh, you don't want to know." "Yes, I want to know." "You really want to know." "Yes, I really want to know." Princess drops her head and looks down, like a little shy girl. "I was just wondering how it feel to be kissed." "What you mean?" Lorenzo inquired. "You know like Clark Gable when he kiss a woman on the movie screen." Lorenzo moves close to Princess, puts his aim around her waist, pulls her close to him, and he kisses her softly and long. Princess felt tingling down her legs and butterflies in her stomach. She pulled away and says "wow" and grabs her head. Lorenzo knew what was happening to her. She was aroused, but he didn't take it any further. Princess said, "I got to get home, let's walk." Lorenzo asked if she was alright. Princess replied, "yeah, I'm okay, I am a little woozy weak in the knees." Lorenzo said, "you'll be alright, you're home now." He plants a kiss on her jaw, she smiled and went into the house. After all her chores are done Princess lays on her bed and reminisces about the long kiss thinking about how Clark Gable kissed his leading lady on the screen in the movies. The next day in school Lorenzo and Princess meet in the hallway. She grabs his hand, looks him dead in the eyes and says, "Do you like me?" "Yes, I like you very much," Lorenzo says. "Am I your girlfriend?" "Yes, Princess you are my girlfriend, the only one."

Della liked Lorenzo, but the feeling wasn't mutual. He talked to Della, but she didn't like her. She was high yellow, sort of cute, but not his type. Della was spreading rumors that she and Lorenzo were girlfriend and boyfriend. Princess got wind of the rumor and confronted Della in the girl's bathroom. "I heard you lying and saying that Lorenzo is your man." Della retorts, "Hey, he is my man." "Hey Della, hey Della, that's a lie he belongs to me. Della lying says, "That's a lie I was with him last night on the school ground. He kissed me and everything. Princess replies, "That cain't be cause he was with me." A crowd of girls has gathered and they are laughing, signifying and taunting Della and Princess. Della slaps Princess. In return, Princess punches Della in the mouth, kicks her in the stomach and pulls her hair. She then slams her head into the wall and hit her in the face. Della's mouth is bleeding, she is dazed and dizzy and she starts to cry and falls to the floor. A teacher heard the commotion and opened the door of a classroom. "What's going on in here?" Miss Jackson, the teacher, is a big solidly built woman. She grabs Princess by the arm and takes her to the Principal's Office. The other girls, who were friends of Della's, tell the Principal that Princess started the fight and that she hit Della first. Princess' mother had to come to school and talk to Professor Brantley. Professor Brantley exclaims, "Princess, I know you are a decent young lady, now tell me what's going on here. Do you wanna tell me what happened, child?" "Yes sir, I guesss." "Well child, speak." Princess begins to cry, puts her head on her mother's shoulder, looks up and dries her eyes. "Della slapped me first." Judy and Janis two of Princess' friends saw the whole fight and confirmed this with Professor Brantley. Prof. Brantley resolved the matter between the girls by talking to Princess and Della. He told them that if there is any more problems between them, he would expel them from class for one month. He also talked to Jewel and Princess and sent Princess home.

Every first Sunday of the month, Princess sings in the program for the Youth Choir. This Sunday, radio station WKBW Chicago is at the church to hear Princess sing. Slick Willie asked them to come and hear Princess hoping they would put her on the radio. Slick Willie was always looking for ways to make more money. Princess sang a solo and the lead in the choir because of her strong, loud voice. The radio station was impressed. Meanwhile, at Lorenzo's house, his mother is listening to the church program on the radio. He hears Princess singing a gospel song, *Our God is the Only God*. She rocks the house. Lorenzo jumps up and hollers, "Ma, that's my girlfriend," with a proud look in his eyes. His mama looks at him in amazement.

Mrs. Perkins, Lorenzo's mother says, "Say, what you say, boy, girlfriend; what you know about a girlfriend?" "Oh nothing, Mom, I was just talking." "What you mean just talking. You better keep your head in those school books for you get in big trouble with these fast ass hot young hussies, you hear me boy. I don't want to have to come up to the school and beat you all the way home for smelling your piss." "Yessum, mother." "Better keep that thing in your pants where it belongs. Don't bring no claps in my house. Lord knows I'll beat you into next week, chile. You finish school get a good job. Help me, your mother, we struggling hard enough. You here trying to bring another mouth to feed, you hear me boy." "Yes ma'am, I hear you." "Now go outside and play."

Three years later, Lorenzo is 18 years old and he receives a letter notifying him that he is to be drafted into the Army. Princess is 17 years old and her sister is 12 years old. Princess sings in nightclubs, chaperoned by her father on Friday and Saturday nights. She makes $100.00 per night. The club is crowded, packed from wall to wall with 200 to 300 people each night at $2.00 a head.

Slick Willie takes advantage of Princess. She gets high and he molests her in the bathroom. He sees blood all over himself and panics, thinking she is hurt. Princess is a virgin and assures Slick Willie she is okay. She cleans up and goes back into the studio booth. She starts singing again, steady thinking about what happened in the bathroom. She feels a bit woozy good, good as the reefer having feeling mellow. She smiles, giggles, feels good and relaxed. She sings her heart out, singing *This is My Last Stop for Love.* She's thinking herself how much she likes Lorenzo and gets a thrill every time she thinks of him.

Lorenzo comes to the studio to see Princess. He knocks on the door and Slick Willie asks him who he's looking for. He says, "My girlfriend." Looking wide eyed, checking everything out, looking all around the studio until he sees Princess in the booth with headphones on. She waves and he waves back. Lorenzo smells a faint smell of reefer. He knows the smell because he and his friends smoke it. Slick Willie closes the door and tells Lorenzo to have a seat. Slick Willie thinks to him who's this nigger coming in here claiming my young piece of trim. I can't let this dude take my young thing away. Then he directs Princess on the song *Is this My Last Stop for Love,* as her eyes meet Lorenzo's she feels so good about Lorenzo, crazy about him.

After the session, Princess and Lorenzo leave the studio. She introduces Lorenzo to Slick Willie. They shake hands and smile the usual nigga phony shit with hate and jealousy in their eyes. One thinking of the other who's getting to Princess. Slick Willie sighs of relief, man if she get pregnant she can put it on Lorenzo. Whew that was a close call. Princess and Lorenzo go to the skating rink on Madison near the video. They were both very good skaters, they learned well from all those falls on the sidewalk growing up. They cruised together smooth as silk, twist and turn figure eights, dips, every smooth move you could do on the floor. They have won several skating contests having fun with their friends.

After skating, Lorenzo and Princess stop and get a famous Vienna red hot sausage, ice cream and a soda. They walk home, eating and laughing. They start dating long and heavy. Lorenzo finally goes to the Army when he sees the date on the letter. After four months of basic training, Lorenzo comes home on thirty days leave before going to Korea in June 1953. He marries Princess and she becomes pregnant. Thirty days later he leaves for Korea. Princess is sad and hurt, she is crying thinking she might not ever see him again. Princess, her sister, mother and some friends of hers and of Lorenzo's go down to Union Street Station to see Lorenzo off to Korea.

Slick Willie thinks that he has a chance to get next to Princess. Princess rejects his advances and tells him if he don't stop bothering her, she'll tell her father about what he did to her at the studio. Slick Willie apologizes and asks for her forgiveness, claiming to be high off the reefer. He then states, "You know how it makes you feel, maybe we can do it again sometimes. Princess says, "Yeah, maybe."

Lorenzo on the ship. The ship was cold going across the Pacific Ocean. The waves were rough coming over into the ship, cold and wet. Many were seasick, vomiting, crying and scared. Some flipped out, thinking about dying.

Some couldn't get off the boat. They put them in brig for court martial for treason. They shot your for treason in the Korea war. Lorenzo prayed every chance he got. He really loved God. He was raised in the church. He thought about dying, but he wasn't afraid of dying. His mother always said out of the body in the presence of the Lord. He had faith in the good Lord Jesus. He was saved when he was 13. Lorenzo, Bob, Larry, and Joe was supposed to go joy riding with John, Eric's brother, but they missed the ride and John took some other boys from the neighborhood with him in his 1951 Chevy. The next morning the headlines in the Chicago Tribune showed a car hitting a gasoline tanker, they all died and burned up. People say you could hear them screaming for mercy, that's when I got saved. I know the Lord will see me through this war.

Lorenzo arrived in Korea. The early morning of June 25, 1953, everybody disembarked off the ship to get settled in for the briefing on the war, where they was supposed to go and wait for the company they were to be assigned to. Everyone was assigned a sleeping bunk in the makeshift barracks, battery powered, along with gasoline generators for back-up. They all chowed down, showered and got a good night's sleep. Lorenzo told his buddy Coleman, "man is sho' feel good to stretch out in a bunk bed after being cramped up on that ship for 25 days. The next morning at 4:00 a.m., Revele, the bugler, blows, "everybody up and at 'em". First Sergeant Jentry, 'all up, right now, this ain't no picnic, all out now"! Everybody scrambles out of bed. Everybody stands by their bunk for head count. Sergeant Jentry is a big burly black dude. He says, "At ease"! Shit, shower, and bath get ready chow, fall out now"! There is a noisy atmosphere in the chow hall. Breakfast consists of powered eggs, bacon, white bread, milk or orange juice. Back at the barracks, head count once again. All beds are shown how to be made up. Everybody goes to lunch. After lunch time, time for the gun range, for combat ready for the front line. It's a known fact that Negros are the first on the front line to be killed. Two weeks of gun range practice, one for briefing, then kill or be killed on the front line.

On Lorenzo's 10th patrol duty at the bottom of Pork Chop Hill, they caught enemy fire, motors and machine gun fire. It was a surprise attack, caught in a crossfire they hit the deck and positioned themselves for a firefight and hand to hand combat. He lost 10 men out of 20. Lorenzo saved the patrol from getting wiped up by singlehandedly taking out three machine guns. He gets wounded by grenade shrapnel but he won't lose his leg. He's been in K. Land for 18 months. He fought on Pork Chop Hill and God was with him. He went to the 38th Parallel, hand to hand combat with the enemy. He saw his buddy get blown to bits right in front of him from a hand grenade. Blew his mind, he has nightmares. They call it shell shock or just plain crazy. In the fox hole late at night Guke Annie would come on the loud speaker, "Hey Joe, Black boy come on over here, fight for us you know the American don't like you. Come on Joe, Black boy we treat you good, we like you, we won't call you nigger. Lots of pretty women, good food, no cold weather, lots of young poontang, you like huh. Come on Joe, Black boy we love you. You know white man hate you." Lorenzo writes to Princess everyday, tells her how much he loves her. He can't wait to get home to see his daughter. He won the Purple Heart for saving his night patrol in the firefight.

Just before he left to come home, Lorenzo and a couple of his buddies went to the cat house that was set up by the government to take the stress off the body, the last goodbye to K. Land. Lorenzo said, "Wow man I kinda hate to leave this place, that thang ain't no joke." Lucas his buddy says, "You right, it's something else, wow but know they love that chocolate stick." They laugh and go back to the barracks to get ready to head home.

They laugh again. Lorenzo laughing, says, "You know, if I could put that thang in a bottle and patent it and put it in a bottle, I'd be rich overnight." They laugh again and walked back to the base.

The next morning, Lorenzo and his buddies board a C147 Transport Troop plane for a ten hour flight back to the States. The plan holds 500 troups. But there's only about 300 soldiers on the plane or less, lot of injured soldiers. There's a curtain between the injured and the soldiers. In front, there is a regular hospital, doctors, nurses, extra pilots, extra crew members, like rafts, lots of rations, in case of an emergency, the plane goes down and hits the water. Everybody is parachuted up with survivor gear just in case. A fuel tanker from the Hawaiian Islands will hook up with the plane in mid-air in the mid-Pacific Ocean to refuel the transport plane for the second half of the nonstop flight to the States. Fighter jets F86 Saber jets escort the planes over Hawaii and turned back to Korea, when the transport plane was in a safe flight pattern. Takeoff is a smooth ride. Ten thousand feet and above the clouds, so quiet and beautiful, moonlight makes it look like daylight.

The next day, they are approaching San Francisco and they see the Golden Gate Bridge. What a beautiful sight. Lorenzo says, "Stateside at last, man, I'm going to kiss the ground when we land. Thank you Jesus." After a prayer with his buddies, they all exchanged addresses and phone numbers and promised to call or write each other.

At Chunete Air Base at 4:00 p.m., the plane lands with 10 carry ons, to pick up troops off plane, ambulances for the sick, fire trucks in case of emergency landing. Everyone stayed overnight for debriefing and the next day they are home bound on the train to Union Downtown Chicago.

Lorenzo has a present for his wife, a Korean Kimono, sandals, some jewelry. Princess was so glad that he sent an allotment check every month, it helped although she was singing and making some money. Even though she had a drug habit, she managed to save $3,000 from the allotment checks. God spared her husband she missed Lorenzo so much. She was so glad she prayed three to five times a day and God heard her prayer. Princess said, "Praise God. Thank you Jesus, amen."

Lorenzo arrives at the Union Station. His mother, sister, brother, Princess and her sister and his baby daughter whom he never laid eyes on to welcome him home. Lorenzo takes his baby daughter in his arms, holds her close to him, kisses her gently and tells her how much he loves her.

Things have changed a lot since Lorenzo has arrived home. Princess lives with her Mom and Pop with her own room, her sister also has her own room. Jim, Princess, and her Dad tell Lorenzo that he can stay with them until he gets a job. He tells Lorenzo that he will help him get a job at the Tribune Towers part-time four hours a night for six months. Lorenzo accepts the job. In the meantime, Lorenzo enrolls in school and gets his G.E.D. diploma. Princess is singing in nightclubs on the weekends, she has been busted for smoking reefer. Lorenzo really loves his wife he'll do anything for her at all costs. He finds out that Princess has a heroin habit. Lord knows Princess is a good woman. She just got caught up in the b.s. He's devastated about her habit. He seeks help from some friends who tells him to put her in the Chicago MD Center in the psych ward for six to eight months.

PRINCESS IS ADMITTED TO THE HOSPITAL.

Lorenzo talks to Princess's father and mother and they all talk to Princess. She agrees to go into the hospital, she knows that it's gonna be a rough ride on kicking the habit. She heard about cold turkey before, all the demons, cold sweats, nightmares, hallucinations, screams, aches and pains, and cramps. Lorenzo, Princess' mom and dad, Lorenzo's mother all go with Princess to the hospital. They all talk to the doctor, he assures them she will get the best of care, the preacher at the church knows the head doctor at the hospital. He treated his son for a heroin habit. He wasn't so lucky, he regressed and died on heroin but he got the best of care in the hospital. All the family, Princess' mom and dad, little sister, Lorenzo's mother, his brother will all chip in to make sure the baby is taken care of while Princess gets well.

Every weekend at least four people went to visit Princess to make sure that she was well loved by her family. Lorenzo never missed a weekend. He remembered all those lonely nights in Korea. How he missed her and prayed that he would get home safe to see his daughter, mother and everyone. He would take Princess a good meal, vegetable soup and fried chicken, greens, corn bread, mac and cheese, Koolade, peach cobbler, rice and gravy. Princess loved to eat, she enjoyed those weekend visits having a picnic on the green lawn in the back of the hospital. Everybody had a picnic on the green on Sunday. Mixed races were there, one side for colored and one side for whites. On Saturday and Sunday the visiting hours were 8:00 a.m. to 4:00 p.m. All family comes on Sunday they all pitch in and pay $5.00 a week for her care.

Lorenzo and Princess go down to the creek to talk. She confesses to him that their daughter might be Slick Willie's. She tells him how Slick Willie took advantage of her with the reefer. He looked at her and paused taking a long deep breath and pulls her close to him, tears in his eyes. She has tears running down her face, they both cry silently, he holds tight, whispers in her ear, "Baby it happens to the best of us, it will be okay baby. I'll make it right," Princess sighs. She dries her eyes, buries her head in her shoulder and sobs silently. Lorenzo puts his hand under her chin and kisses her gently and says, "Is this our last stop for love?" Princess says, "Yes, baby this is our last stop for love, I love you Daddy." "Yes, baby I love you too", says Lorenzo. They walk, hug and kiss back too family gathering. She picks up her daughter and sighs to himself, "My little queen." Everybody is chattering almost to time to go they all hug and kiss Princess, laugh and cry a little. Princess goes back inside.

On Saturday and Sunday evenings, Princess entertains her fellow patients in the auditorium. There is every kind of so-called crazy patient in this hospital. Depression drugs, so-called schizo, the prescription drugs makes their problems worse, but everyone seems to hold their own. Four patients that are kicking the heroin habit have a four piece band. They are a professional group and are there under assumed names. The band consists of a drum set, two guitars, rhythm and bass. They help Princess with her songs, practicing with her and helping her with her notes and range. She sang five songs both on Saturday and Sunday night. The four would play an hour set each night. Princess' favorite song is *Is This My Last Stop for Love.* When she sings it, tears come to her eyes thinking about Lorenzo. Princess only knows the guys played with as Joe, Bob, Sam and John. They were a well known group due to the situation they were in they didn't want the public to know anything about their stay in the hospital.

The first night they gave Princess some methadone and put her in a padded cell so she wouldn't hurt herself. She experienced pain, hallucinations, stomach cramps and severe vomiting. She had a rough night, nightmares, urinating, defecating, crying and bumping her head on the wall. Round midnight, they gave her a sedative, put her on an eight hour watch, and removed the straitjacket so she could relax. She slept all through the night, was closely watched on orders of the Head Doctor no b.s. or he would release her the next day.

Dr. Johnson, a Swede was color blind who believed in human rights. They don't play racism in his country, he is loved and hated by the staff, Black and white staff, orderlies, LPNs, janitors, kitchen help alike. Dr. Johnson is 6'5 V2" with blond hair. He is very masculine, muscular, with striking features. He is a straight shooter down the middle and really believes in fairness.

The next day Princess wakes up feeling groggy. Her cell is a mess, feces on her and the floor, vomit on the floor, bed and all in her hair. Two female nurses come in and put her in a wheel chair half nude and looking wild.

They take to her to the shower, clean her up, and fix her hair. They take her to the chow hall in a wheel chair. Everyone is looking at her, some smiled, others nodded in acceptance. She tries to eat but cannot hold anything down in her stomach. She drinks a half glass of milk, some rice and chicken. She wraps a couple of pieces in her napkin and she puts in her pocket. She takes it back to her room for a late night snack.

Eight months have gone by, Princess, a model patient, is released from the hospital. Lorenzo greets her, she smiles, they hug and kiss a long kiss. Princess is glad to be home. Lorenzo gets a G.I. home loan to buy a restaurant. Lorenzo's brother is a numbers runner both live on the Southside of Chicago where all the so-called high class Negros live, the ones who can afford to live there. Lorenzo lends his brother the money to buy a plush nightclub. His wife Princess' sister hooks up Lorenzo's brother. They hung together went clubbing together and dancing. Princess sang in the club. She is surprised one night when she comes to the club and her old friends from the hospital are there. Her husband invited them to come and play with Princess. They tore the house down. Everybody was grooving until the wee hours.

Lorenzo's brother had the hookup with the crooked Chicago police. They would take a bribe at the drop of a hat. Gangsters come to the club to collect money from

Lorenzo's brother. Brian tells the gangsters that he doesn't have the money. Before they leave, they tell him he better have the money in two days or else he'll have a problem. The gangsters send some crooked cops to shut the club down until they get their money. They think Brian is holding out on the numbers money. The Bug Man they call him, had a thyroid problem. He confronts Brian about the money, that his brother borrowed from him they almost fought. His brother had his boys with him ten deep and strapped, he was talking plenty shit. Brian told Bug Man, "You gonna come down here to Nigger Town with your wop ass and take out money. I don't think so. We own this Niggerville here and we ain't giving up shit period. Better take your white asses outta here. We ain't giving up shit, we have to eat just like you. You shoot us we gonna shoot back, and you can't come down here and collect, cause you don't where to collect." Bug Man angrily replied, "You win nigger this time." Brian counters with, "Mister Nigger to you wop muthafucka. Yeah we win, we gonna keep winnin' you wop peckerwoods don't scare nobody." Bug Man tells his boys to go because these niggers are crazy. Lorenzo gives Bug Man the money his brother owed. As Bug Man leaves he says, "I'll see ya'll later," and uses his fingers like a tommy gun as he shouts, "tat, tat, tat, tat." Lorenzo and his brother laugh and reply, "tat, tat, tat, tat to ya." When Bug Man leaves, Lorenzo, his brother and his boys crack up laughing. Lorenzo says, "You see that look on that wop cracker's face, ha, ha, ha, ha. Yeah we ain't scared of no honky wop." Lorenzo, his brother and their families leave ChiTown with $100,000 stashed in their spare tire heading for Los Angeles.

1954–1958

Lorenzo goes into the record business. Lorenzo and Princess have another child, a girl. Princess is still singing in clubs and signs a recording contract with Stax Records. Princess has been clean of her habit for several years now. She loves Lorenzo. They have come a long way through thick and thin. They are on top of their game and have a big beautiful home, three car garage, maids and a nanny for their newborn child. The song *Is This My Last Stop for Love* is playing in the background. Lorenzo is a producer and he has Slick Willie to help. "Slick Willie, don't go near Princess," Lorenzo says, after his boys put a country whopping on Slick Willie's Black ass, "or face rape charges or get killed by Princess' father." So he took the ass whopping like a man. After it was over, everything was squashed, mum's the word.

Lorenzo is producing gospel and R&B recordings for top Black artists and selling their contracts to the big record companies, Columbia, Capital, Stax, and other companies.

By the early sixties, Lorenzo, Princess, their children and their parents are living the good life in California. Princess is singing *Is This My Last Stop for Love* as she and Lorenzo are walking in their garden with their children as they watch the California sun fading into the horizon.

THE END

Printed in the United States
By Bookmasters